The Red Badge of Courage

Retold from the Stephen Crane
original by Oliver Ho

Illustrated by Jamel Akib

STERLING

New York / London
www.sterlingpublishing.com/kids

STERLING and the distinctive Sterling logo are registered trademarks of
Sterling Publishing Co., Inc.

Library of Congress Cataloging-in-Publication Data Available

4 6 8 10 9 7 5

Published by Sterling Publishing Co., Inc.
387 Park Avenue South, New York, NY 10016
Copyright © 2006 by Oliver Ho
Illustrations copyright © 2006 by Jamel Akib
Distributed in Canada by Sterling Publishing
^{c}/$_o$ Canadian Manda Group, 165 Dufferin Street
Toronto, Ontario, Canada M6K 3H6
Distributed in the United Kingdom by GMC Distribution Services
Castle Place, 166 High Street, Lewes, East Sussex, England, BN7 1XU
Distributed in Australia by Capricorn Link (Australia) Pty. Ltd.
P.O. Box 704, Windsor, NSW 2756, Australia

Classic Starts is a trademark of Sterling Publishing Co., Inc.

Printed in China
All rights reserved
Designed by Renato Stanisic

Sterling ISBN 978-1-4027-2663-7

For information about custom editions, special sales, premium and
corporate purchases, please contact Sterling Special Sales
Department at 800-805-5489 or specialsales@sterlingpublishing.com.

CONTENTS

CHAPTER 1

A Rumor of Battle

ᥫᩣ

The cold passed slowly from the earth. The moving fog revealed an army dressed in blue resting on the hills. As the soldiers woke up, they could see more of the muddy roads and the river. A tall soldier went to wash his shirt and came running back with a story he had heard.

"We're going to move tomorrow," he said. "We're going up the river. We'll cross over it and come around behind them."

"I don't believe it," another private said loudly. "I've been ready to move eight times in

1

the last two weeks, and we haven't moved yet."

While the men continued to argue about whether or not they would be moving the next day, a young private named Henry Fleming went to his hut to be alone and think. It amazed him to think that there could be a battle so soon. And he would be in it! It would be one of those great affairs of the earth.

Henry had dreamed of battles and of being a hero all his life, but he had never thought he would actually be in a war. Back at home, he hadn't believed the war was real. He thought that men were better now, or at least more peaceful than they had been in the past. Surely they would not go to war. But now they were fighting a civil war, the North against the South! This was his chance to be a hero.

Henry had wanted to enlist several times, but his mother had discouraged him. She had given him a hundred reasons why he was needed more on the farm than on the field of battle. Finally, when he couldn't wait any longer, he went into town and joined up. When he told her, she said, "The Lord's will be done, Henry," and then she continued to milk the cow. "You watch out and take care of yourself. Don't go thinking you can beat the whole rebel army right away. You're just one little fellow among a lot of others."

She told him to watch out for bad men who would curse or do other things that would make her ashamed of him. "I don't know what else to tell you," she said. "Except that you must never avoid your duty on my account. If there comes a time when you have to be killed to do the right thing, Henry, don't think of anything except doing what's right."

His spirits had soared on the way to Washington. The troop was treated so well as they traveled that he already felt as if he was a hero. Then, after many difficult journeys and long pauses, there had come months of boring life in a camp. Here there were no death struggles. All the men did was try to keep warm and do practice drills over and over again. All he thought about during this time was the battles to come.

Henry didn't much care about what kind of men he would fight. There was a more serious problem. He wanted to know that he wouldn't run from battle. He had never needed to think about this before, but now a battle was really going to happen and he realized that he might run. As far as war was concerned, he didn't know anything about himself.

After a time, the tall soldier entered the hut. He was followed by the loud private who had disagreed with him earlier. They were still fighting. The tall soldier was named Jim

Conklin. The loud one was called Wilson.

"That's all right," said Jim as he entered, waving his hand. "You can believe me or not. All you've got to do is sit and wait. Pretty soon you'll find out I was right."

"Well, you just know everything in the world, don't you?" said Wilson.

"Didn't say I knew everything in the world," said Jim sharply. He began to pack his belongings into his knapsack.

Henry watched them nervously and finally asked, "Going to be a battle for sure then, is there, Jim?"

"Of course there is," replied Jim. "You just wait until tomorrow and you'll see one of the biggest battles ever. You just wait."

He talked about the other troops and the battles he had heard about. Then Henry asked how their own troop would do.

"Oh, they'll fight all right, I guess. Once they get into it," said Jim, with cold judgment. "Everyone makes fun of them because they're new, but they'll be all right."

"Think any of the boys'll run?" asked Henry.

"Oh, there may be a few," said Jim. "There's that kind in every troop, especially when they first go under fire. You can't bet on anything, but I think they'll fight better than some, worse than others."

"Do you ever think you might run yourself, Jim?" Henry asked, and then laughed as if he meant it as a joke. He didn't want to anger his friend.

"Well, I've thought it might get too hot for old Jim Conklin," Jim said. "And if a whole lot of boys run, why I suppose I'll run, too. And once I start, I'll run like the devil. But if everybody is standing and fighting, why I'll stand and fight. I'll bet on it."

Henry felt happy to hear those words. He had thought that all of the other untried men were very sure of themselves. Now that he knew the truth, he felt a little better.

CHAPTER 2

Henry's Fears

The next morning Henry discovered that Jim had been wrong. There was no battle that day. A lot of the other men made fun of Jim. He even got into a fistfight with a man from Chatfield Corners. The loud soldier, Wilson, also got into a fight, and the lieutenant had to break it up. Meanwhile, Henry still felt unsure of himself.

For days he thought it over. He was still worried that he would run at the first sign of a fight. Finally he decided that the only way to prove himself would be to go into the blaze. He would just have to wait and see if he actually fought. So he waited for an opportunity and tried to compare himself to his friends.

Jim made Henry feel much better. He seemed so unworried, and appeared confident in himself. Nothing seemed to be beyond his ability. When Henry studied the other soldiers, he sometimes thought that they were all heroes. Surely they were all better than he could ever hope to be. At other times he thought they were just as nervous and uncertain as he was.

One morning, Henry was standing with the rest of his troop. Everyone was whispering and telling one another the old rumors again. They were sure there would be a battle soon. In the gloom before daybreak, their uniforms glowed a deep blue color. The sun was about to rise, and the huge figure of the colonel on a horse loomed against the yellow patch of sky. The troop stood for what seemed like a long time and Henry grew impatient.

At last, another man on a horse rode toward them. The soldiers nearby tried to listen as he spoke with the colonel. After a few minutes, the second man turned his horse around and rode away. A moment later, the troop went marching off into the darkness. It was now like a moving monster with many feet. The air was heavy and cold with dew. The mass of wet grass, when marched on, rustled like silk.

The sun rose, and Henry saw that the landscape was streaked with two long, thick, black columns. The columns disappeared over a hill in front of them and vanished into the woods behind them. They were lines of men marching to battle, but they looked like two snakes crawling from the cavern of the night.

The river wasn't in view, and the soldiers continued to fight about what the plans could be. Henry took no part in the fights. As he walked, he kept asking himself whether or not he would run. He couldn't stop thinking about it. He looked ahead, often expecting to hear the sound of firing guns.

The other men had begun to joke and laugh. Some of them even sang. Henry felt cut off from the others. At nightfall, the column broke into separate troops. Each troop went into the fields to camp. Tents sprang up like strange plants, and campfires dotted the night like red flowers.

CHAPTER 3

A Conversation with a Friend

Henry walked by himself in the darkness. He lay down in the grass and felt sorry for himself. He wished he was at home again, making the rounds from the house to the barn, the barn to the fields, the fields to the barn, and the barn to the house. Henry remembered how he had often yelled at the cows and her mates, but now he thought of them with happiness. He told himself he wasn't made to be a soldier, and thought about how different he was from the other men in his troop.

Henry heard the rustle of grass. He looked around, saw the loud soldier, and called out, "Oh, Wilson!"

"Why, hello, Henry," said Wilson. "Is that you? What are you doing here?"

"Oh, just thinking," said Henry.

Wilson began talking about the fight they thought they would be in soon.

"Oh, we've got them now!" he said. "At last, we'll get them good."

"Well, Jim Conklin says we'll get plenty of fighting," said Henry.

"He's right for once, I guess. We're in for a big battle. That's for certain," said Wilson.

"You're going to do great things, I suppose," said Henry.

"Oh, I don't know," said Wilson. "I guess I'll do as well as the rest. I'm going to try like thunder."

"How do you know you won't run when the time comes?" asked Henry.

"Run?" said Wilson, and he laughed. "Run? Of course I won't run."

"Well, a lot of good men thought they were going to do great things before the fight," said Henry. "But when the time came, they ran away."

"That's true, I guess," said Wilson. "But I'm not going to do that. The man that bets on my running will lose his money."

"Oh, shucks," said Henry. "Are you the bravest man in the world?"

"No, I'm not," said Wilson. "And I didn't say I was, either. I said I was going to do my share of fighting. And I am, too. Who are you to talk to me like that, anyhow?"

He glared at Henry for a moment and then walked away. Henry yelled after him, "Well, you don't need to get mad about it!"

Henry felt alone and miserable. No one else seemed to be struggling with whether or not he would run. He felt like an outsider. He went back to his tent and lay on a blanket next to Jim, who was snoring. In the darkness, Henry saw visions of fear that would make him run away while others stayed and fought. He knew that he wouldn't be able to deal with this monster. He stared at the reflection of a fire on the wall of his tent until, tired and sick of worrying, he fell asleep.

CHAPTER 4

A Letter from Wilson

Another night came and the columns of men crossed two bridges. Henry was sure that they would be attacked from the caves in the woods at any moment. But no one bothered them in their camping place, and the soldiers slept the brave sleep of tired men. In the morning they woke up early and ran along a narrow road that led deep into the forest.

The men began to count the miles. Many threw away their knapsacks. Soon, few carried anything but their necessary clothes, blankets, canteens, guns, and ammunition.

"You can now eat and shoot," said Jim to Henry. "That's all you want to do."

They marched on and on for a few days, and Henry began to think of this as nothing but a demonstration of men in blue uniforms showing how well they could march.

One gray dawn, however, he was kicked in the leg by Jim. Before he was even fully awake, Henry found himself running down a road among men who were panting from moving so fast. From far ahead of them came the sudden sputter of firing guns. They were running right toward it!

Henry was confused. He tried to think as he ran with his friends, but all he knew was that the men behind would run him over if he fell. He needed to focus in order to keep from tripping.

He felt as if he was being carried along by a mob.

One by one, other troops came into view. Henry knew that his time had come. He was about to be tested. Looking around, he saw that it would be impossible to escape from the troop. They were on all sides. He felt as if he was in a moving box. Henry realized that he had never wanted to come to the war. He felt as if he hadn't chosen to join the army. He had been dragged in by the government, who had made him feel that it was his duty to come, and now they were taking him out to be killed. He felt angry for being here. He didn't trust the people who were in charge of the army.

When the men arrived at the clearing, Henry expected to see a battle scene. Instead, there were a few groups of men running back and forth. They were firing at the landscape. A flag fluttered. The troop passed a dead body, and the wind raised the man's beard as if a hand were stroking it.

Strange ideas took hold of Henry as he marched on and on. He thought the land threatened him. At any moment the enemy would attack, killing him and his friends. He wanted to warn them that the generals didn't know what they were doing, but he knew that no one would listen. They would probably laugh.

When they stopped and lay on the ground for safety, many of the men in the troop began building tiny hills in front of them. They used stones, sticks, earth, and anything else they thought might stop a bullet. The men discussed whether this was honorable or not—whether it would be more honorable to stand and face the enemy without protection. The troop was ordered to move again and again, which made Henry impatient. He wondered out loud why they were doing this.

Jim ate a little and answered, "Oh, I suppose we must go walking around to keep them from getting too close, or something."

In the afternoon the troop went out over the same ground it had walked in the morning. The land was more familiar to Henry. It didn't threaten him anymore. But any time they passed into a new region, his old worries of stupidity and fear came back to him. After a while, he decided that the stupidity didn't matter much. He wondered what it would be like to get shot right away in his first battle.

Soon Henry heard guns ahead. He saw the soldiers running, followed by the sound of gunfire. Henry forgot about getting shot. He watched the battle, spellbound. Suddenly he felt a heavy

hand on his shoulder. He turned and saw the loud soldier, Wilson.

"It's my first and last battle, old boy," Wilson said. He was very pale and his lip was trembling.

"Eh?" murmured Henry, in great astonishment.

"I said it's my first and last battle. Something tells me——"

"What?" asked Henry.

"I want you to take these here things to my folks," he said, and ended with a little sob of pity for himself. He handed Henry a small envelope.

"Why, what the devil..." began Henry.

But the other man gave him a glance as from the depths of a tomb, raised his limp hand, and turned away.

CHAPTER 5

The Battle Begins

〜

The men were stopped at the edge of a grove. They crouched among the trees, pointed their restless guns out at the fields, and tried to look beyond the smoke. Out of the haze they could see other men running. Some shouted and gestured as they ran. The men in Henry's troop watched and listened eagerly. They kept busy by talking about the rumors they had heard.

"I met one of the boys from Maine," one of the men said. "He says his brigade fought the whole rebel army for four hours and killed about five thousand of them. He says one more fight like that and the war will be over."

The noise in front of them grew, and Henry and his friends were frozen into silence. They could see a flag waving angrily in the smoke. Near it were the blurred shapes of troops. A confused stream of men fled across the fields.

A shell screaming like a storm went over the heads of the reserves. It landed in the grove and exploded, flinging brown earth and a shower of pine needles everywhere. Bullets began to whistle among the branches and nip at the trees. Twigs and leaves came sailing down. It was as if a thousand small invisible axes were flying at them. Many of the men had to dodge and duck their heads.

The lieutenant of Henry's company was shot in the hand. He cursed so much that a nervous laugh went through the troop. He held his wound carefully so no blood would drip onto his pants. Then the captain of the company wrapped a handkerchief around the wound.

The battle flag in the distance waved about madly. It seemed to be struggling to free itself. The swirling smoke was filled with horizontal flashes. Men running quickly away from the fight appeared to come out of the smoke. They grew in numbers until it was obvious that the whole troop was fleeing. The flag suddenly sank down as if dying. Its motion as it fell seemed to be a sign of despair.

The looks on the faces of the men running away scared Henry. He felt like nothing in the world would hold him still if he was given the chance to run. But the men in his troop had to hold their ground. They stood together as a group, shaking and growing pale.

Henry had one little thought in the middle of all this chaos. The monster that had made the other troops flee had not yet appeared. He decided to get a look at it. If he could do that, he thought, he might run faster than anyone else.

CHAPTER 6

The First Shot

⤜∽

There were many moments of waiting. Henry's thoughts drifted to the street at home when everyone was waiting for the springtime circus parade to begin.

Suddenly someone cried, "Here they come!"

There was rustling and muttering among the men. They pulled boxes of bullets around them and shifted their positions with great care.

"Here they come! Here they come!" Gunlocks clicked.

Across the smoke-covered field came a swarm

of men in gray uniforms, yelling loudly and shrilly. As he caught sight of them, Henry was suddenly troubled by the thought that his gun might not be loaded. He tried to remember when he had loaded it, but he was too nervous.

A hatless general pulled his horse to a stand near the colonel of Henry's troop. He shook his fist in the other's face.

"You've got to hold them back!" he shouted angrily. "You've got to hold them back!"

In his nervousness, the colonel began to stammer.

"A-all r-right, General, by God! We-we'll d-d-do—do our best, General."

The general made a passionate gesture and rode away. The man at Henry's elbow was mumbling, as if to himself, "Oh, we're in for it now! We're in for it now!"

The captain of the company was pacing excitedly back and forth behind the men. He kept repeating, "Hold your fire, boys. Don't shoot until I tell you. Wait until they get close up."

Henry took one look at the enemy in the field in front of him and stopped wondering if his gun was loaded. Before he was ready—before he had told himself that he was about to fight—he threw his rifle into position. He fired a first wild shot even before the order came, and continued working his weapon.

He suddenly lost all concern for himself. He felt as if he was part of something larger. The only thing he knew was that whatever he was now a part of was in trouble. He could no more leave his troop than a little finger could leave a hand. He was always aware of his friends beside him. It was a brotherhood born of the smoke and danger of death.

CHAPTER 7

Fighting, at Last

Henry worked quickly and a burning roar filled his ears. Once the roar passed, he felt a red rage, like that of a cornered and driven beast. He fought frantically. The men around him were all making strange noises. No one was in a heroic pose—they were too busy loading, firing, and reloading their rifles.

The officers stood behind the men and encouraged them. The lieutenant in Henry's company came across a soldier who had run when the firing began. He quickly grabbed the man by the collar and forced him to return to the front line. The soldier went, but it was clear that his heart was not in the fight. He tried to reload his gun, but his hands shook too much and the lieutenant had to help him.

The men dropped here and there like bundles. The captain of Henry's company had been killed in an early part of the action. His body lay stretched out like a man resting, but his face had a surprised and sorrowful look, as if he had been killed not by the enemy, but by a friend. A man who was crying near Henry had been grazed by a shot that made blood stream down his face.

At last a yell went along the line and the firing died down. As the smoke cleared, Henry saw that the men in gray had been pushed back. The enemy was scattered in groups. Some in his troop began to shout. Many were silent. As the fever left him, Henry thought he was going to choke.

He was dirty and dripping with sweat. He took a long, cold drink from his canteen.

"We've held them back!" someone yelled.

Henry was joyous. Around him lay many bodies, as if they had fallen from the sky. Henry saw battles going on in the distance and was surprised to realize that he hadn't been in the center of the only battle.

As he looked around, Henry noticed the blue sky and the sun shining on the trees and fields. It was amazing to him that nature had gone on in the middle of so much war.

CHAPTER 8

The Men Flee

Henry looked around in a daze. He picked up his cap from the ground, wiggled in his jacket to make it more comfortable, and bent down to retie his shoelaces.

So it was over at last! The test had been passed and the difficulties of war had been beaten. Henry was thrilled. He was sure that he had been wonderful. The other men in his troop seemed to feel just as proud of themselves. They shook hands and helped the ones who were hurt. But suddenly, cries of amazement broke out among the troops.

"Here they come again!" someone yelled.

Henry saw forms running out of the woods in the distance. He saw the tilted flag speeding forward.

The shells, which hadn't bothered the troop for some time, came swirling around them again. They exploded in the grass and among the trees. The explosions looked like strange flowers bursting into fierce bloom.

The men groaned. They moved slowly and stiffly. As they watched the rapid approach of the enemy, they began to rebel against their duty.

"Why can't somebody send support?" someone asked.

"We won't survive a second attack," said another. "I didn't come to fight the whole darned rebel army myself."

Henry stared. Surely, he thought, this was not about to happen. There could not be another battle. He waited as if everyone would stop and admit that it was a mistake. But the firing began again and ripped in both directions. Henry's neck was shaking and his hands were awkward. He began to imagine that the enemy men were better and stronger than the men in his troop. The enemy must be machines of steel. In the smoke they looked like dragons.

A man near him who had been working busily at his rifle suddenly stopped and ran away with a loud howl. Another, who had worn an expression of courage, saw this and became afraid. He, too, threw down his gun and fled. There was no shame in his face. He ran like a rabbit.

Others began to hurry away through the smoke. Henry watched them, yelled with fright, and turned around. He started running.

For a moment he lost the direction of safety.

Death and injury threatened him from every direction. He began to speed toward the back of the troop. His rifle and cap were gone. His unbuttoned coat blew in the wind. On his face was all the horror of his imagination. The lieutenant tried to catch him, but Henry escaped. He ran like a blind man. Once, he knocked his shoulder into a tree so hard that he fell over.

As soon as Henry turned his back on the enemy, his fears grew even greater. His imagination made everything worse. As he ran, he saw men on his right and left doing the same. He heard many footsteps behind him. Shells flew over his head with long wild screams.

Henry was amazed when he came within view of another troop of men in action. They were fighting with great enthusiasm. No one seemed to know the death that was headed their way. Henry thought they were fools and pitied them.

He kept moving toward the back of the action. Finally, Henry saw a general sitting on a horse. Sometimes the general was surrounded by other men on horses. At other times he was alone.

Henry stayed near the general and tried to overhear what he was saying. Perhaps the general would ask him for information. Henry could tell him about all the confusion on the front lines. He knew all about it. He wanted to tell the general that it was wrong to sit here and make no effort to stop the death happening behind him. Any fool could see that the men should pull back.

One of the officers rode up to the general and said, "By heavens, they have! They've held them!"

The general began to roar at his troops, "We've got them now! We've got them for sure!"

CHAPTER 9

The Man in the Forest

‿♋

Henry flinched, as if discovered in a crime. They had won after all! The fools who had stayed behind had beaten the enemy. He could hear cheering behind him. He turned away, amazed and angry. He felt that he had been wronged.

He had fled, he told himself, because total defeat was coming. He had done a good thing by saving himself. Henry was a little piece of the army, and it was the duty of every little piece to rescue itself if it could. Later, the officers could fit the little pieces back together to make a whole army again. His actions had been wise, Henry assured himself.

Thoughts of his friends came to him. They had held strong and won. This thought made Henry grow bitter. It seemed that their foolishness had betrayed him. He thought he had done the smart thing by running, and now he felt a great anger at his friends who had not done the same.

Henry knew that his friends would make fun of him when he returned to camp. He began to pity himself when he thought of how badly they would treat him. He left the field and went into a thick patch of woods. He wanted to get away from hearing the few shots that were still being fired.

The ground was covered with vines and bushes, and the trees grew close together. Henry had to force his way through. The thorns from the bushes tore at his legs, and the branches blocked the way. Henry couldn't make peace with the forest. He made so much noise that he was afraid other men would hear him. He went far into the forest, looking for a dark place where he could be alone. After a time, the sound of gunfire grew faint. The cannons boomed far in the distance. The sun blazed among the trees. The insects were making noises in a rhythm. They seemed to be grinding their teeth in unison. A woodpecker worked at the side of a tree, and a bird flew by.

Far away was the rumble of death, but here Henry could only hear the sounds of nature.

This landscape made him feel better. It was peaceful. A pinecone fell from a tree and landed near a squirrel, which quickly ran away. Henry saw that this was the law of nature. The squirrel had understood that there was danger and had taken to its legs right away.

Henry went farther into the deep forest.

Finally he reached a place where the high, curved branches seemed to form a chapel. Pine needles made a gentle brown carpet and there was a soft light.

Near the entrance he stopped, shocked at the sight before him.

In front of Henry sat a dead man with his back against a tree. The man was dressed in a uniform that had once been blue, but was now faded to a sad shade of green. The eyes that were staring at Henry had changed to a dull color, like the side of a fish. The mouth was open. Its once red lips had changed to a terrible yellow. Little ants ran over the man's gray skin. One was carrying some sort of bundle along his upper lip.

Henry gave a shriek as he saw the body. He couldn't move or turn his eyes away from the man. It was as if he had been turned to stone for a few moments. He stared into the strange eyes. Slowly, Henry put one hand behind him and

rested it against a tree. Leaning on this, he drew back step-by-step, his face still looking toward the man. He was scared that if he turned his back the body might jump up and chase after him.

The branches pushed against Henry and threatened to knock him over. His feet caught in the vines. He imagined touching the body and shook terribly.

At last he broke free of the branches and vines, and fled. He didn't watch where he was going. He just ran. In his imagination, Henry was being chased by the sight of the black ants crawling on the gray face.

After a time, he paused and listened. He was out of breath from running. Henry imagined some strange voice would come from the dead man's throat and yell after him.

Behind him, the trees around the body moved in a soft wind. There was a sad silence.

CHAPTER 10

The Tattered Man

The sun sank, and there was a pause in the noise of the insects. In the middle of this stillness, there suddenly came a great clash of sounds. Henry stopped and listened. A roar came from the distance. He heard the ripping sound of gunfire and the breaking crash of cannons.

Henry's mind flew in all directions. He imagined the two armies were still fighting. After listening for a long time, he began to run in the direction of the battle. Henry knew that it was strange for him to run toward battle when he had just worked so hard to be away from it. But he told himself that if the earth and moon were about to crash, many people would get up on their roofs to watch it happen. He felt the same way about the battle. He didn't want to miss an event that people would be talking about for years to come.

As he ran, it occurred to Henry that the fight he had been in was, after all, nothing but a warm up. When he listened to the sounds of the battle going on now, he doubted that he had ever seen a real fight. It was almost funny to him. He and his friends had taken the enemy very seriously and imagined that they were deciding the war. They all thought they were going to be heroes, but the truth was that they would hardly be mentioned at all.

Henry hurried forward, imagining all kinds of battle scenes. The vines and branches tried to hold him back and block his way, but he got through it all. Soon he could see long gray walls of smoke. The sounds of the cannons shook him. He was shocked at the noise and stared in the direction of the fight.

Finally Henry continued forward. The battle sounded like the grinding of a terrible machine. It was amazing to hear, but he would have to get closer to see it.

He came to a road where a crowd of wounded men was walking slowly away from the battle. They were cursing, groaning, and crying. One of the men carried a shoe full of blood. He hopped like a schoolboy and laughed as if he was crazy. Another was singing in a high and shaky voice. Many of the men were angry. A few of them helped carry an officer who was yelling orders to the men closest to him.

Henry joined this crowd and marched along with it. A tattered-looking man walked quietly at his side. He was covered with dust and blood, and had gunpowder stains from his hair to his shoes. He was listening to a sergeant who was talking to him. After a time the tattered man moved closer to Henry and tried to talk. Henry saw that the man had two wounds, one in the arm and one in the head, which was bound with a blood-soaked rag. The tattered man's voice was gentle, and his eyes seemed to begging for something.

"It was a pretty good fight, wasn't it?" he asked.

Henry, deep in thought, glanced up at the bloody and grim figure.

"What?"

"A pretty good fight, wasn't it?" the man asked.

"Yes," said Henry. He started walking faster, but the other man limped after him.

"I've never seen men fight like that," the

tattered man said. "How they did fight! I knew our boys would be tough once they started fighting. I knew it would turn out this way. You can't beat our boys, no sir. They're fighters, that's for sure."

He looked at Henry for encouragement several times, but Henry didn't respond. The tattered man kept talking.

"I was talking across the line with a boy from Georgia, in the enemy army. He said we would run as soon as the gunfire started. I said we wouldn't do it. I said maybe *his* men would run and he laughed. Well, nobody ran today, did they? Everybody fought and fought and fought."

His face had a look that was like love for the army. After a time, he asked Henry, "Where are you hit, my boy?"

Henry felt an instant panic at this question.

"What?" he asked.

"Where are you hit?" the man asked again.

"Why," began Henry. "I—I—that is—why, I—"

Suddenly he turned away and ran through the crowd. His face was red, and his fingers picked nervously at one of his buttons. He kept his head down and stared at the button as if there was a problem with it.

CHAPTER 11

Jim Conklin

∽

Henry fell to the back of the crowd and stayed out of sight until the tattered soldier was gone. Then he started to walk on with the others. But he was among wounded men. The tattered soldier's question had made him feel that his shame could be seen by everyone. At times he looked at the other men with envy. He wished that he, too, had a wound. A red badge of courage.

There was an injured man at the side of the road. The other men were trying to help him, but he turned them away and told them to leave him alone. His face was gray and his lips tight. He moved stiffly, as if he was trying to protect his wounds. As he walked, he seemed to be looking for a place to stop. He looked like someone choosing a gravesite.

Something in the way the man waved the other soldiers away startled Henry. He yelled in horror. He laid a hand on the man's arm and, when he turned, Henry cried, "Jim Conklin!"

Jim gave Henry a little smile.

"Hello, Henry," he said.

"Oh, Jim, oh, Jim, oh, Jim," Henry said.

"Where have you been, Henry?" Jim asked, and held out his hand. "I was worried about you."

Henry could only say, "Oh, Jim."

"You know," Jim said. "I was out there. What a circus! And I got shot—I got shot. It's real bad."

As the two friends marched on, Jim suddenly seemed to be overcome with fear. He grabbed Henry's arm and began to speak in a shaky whisper. Henry could see that his friend was very weak.

"I'll tell you what I'm afraid of, Henry. I'm afraid I'll fall down and they'll either leave me here, or one of those artillery wagons will ride right over me."

Henry cried out, "I'll take care of you, Jim! I swear I will."

Jim hung on Henry's arm.

"I was always a good friend to you, wasn't I, Henry?" he asked. "I've always been a good person. And it isn't too much to ask, is it? Just to pull me away from the road? I would do it for you, Henry."

Henry couldn't say anything, and Jim walked away from him.

Henry followed his friend. Soon he heard a voice at his shoulder. Turning, he saw the tattered soldier.

"You should take him out of the road,

partner," the tattered soldier said. "There's a wagon coming and he'll get run over."

Henry ran to his friend and tried to pull him off the road. Jim tried to get away for a moment, and then said, "Oh! Into the fields?"

Jim started running through the grass, and Henry ran after him. He yelled for Jim to stop, but he kept running. It amazed Henry that his friend still had such strength.

"Where are you going, Jim?" Henry asked, with a shaky voice. "What are you thinking about? What are you doing?"

Jim turned and said, "Leave me alone, can't you?"

"Why, Jim?" Henry asked in a dazed way. "What's the matter with you?"

Jim turned and ran forward. Henry and the tattered soldier followed, surprised and afraid. It seemed like part of a religious ceremony. At last they saw Jim stop and stand still. He seemed to be waiting patiently for something that he had come to meet.

There was a silence.

Finally, Jim's chest began to heave and he sank to the ground.

Henry turned with sudden anger toward the battlefield. He shook his fist and seemed about to yell.

Above him, the red sun was pasted in the sky like a wafer.

CHAPTER 12

The Tattered Man's Question

❧

The tattered man stood, thinking.

"Well, he was a sight, wasn't he?" he finally said in a surprised voice. "I wonder where he got his strength from. I've never seen a man run like that after he's been shot a few times. It was a funny thing."

Henry wanted to cry out, but he couldn't make a sound. The tattered man stood and watched him.

"Look here, partner," he said after a time. "Your friend's gone, isn't he? You might as well look out for number one. Nobody's going to bother your friend anymore. And I must say, I'm not enjoying any great health myself these days."

Henry looked up at him quickly. He saw that the tattered soldier was swaying uncertainly on his legs, and his face had turned a strange shade of blue.

"Not you too," Henry cried. "You're not going—"

The man waved his hand.

"Nah, all I want is some pea soup and a good bed," he said.

They started walking back to the road. For a time they moved quietly. Finally the tattered man said, "You know, partner, I'm starting to feel pretty bad."

Henry groaned. He wondered if he was going to see another grim display. But his new friend reassured him.

"Oh, I'm not going yet," he said. "I've got too

much to take care of. You should see how many children I've got."

Henry could see the shadow of a smile on the tattered man's face. He had been making a joke.

They walked a little longer and the tattered man talked about his hometown. Then he said rather calmly, "I don't believe I can walk much farther. You look pretty tired yourself. I bet you're worse off than you think. You should take care of your wound. It's not good to leave these things alone. Where is it?"

Henry had been hoping the man wouldn't bring up this topic again. He now gave a cry of anger and made a furious motion with his hand.

"Oh, don't bother me!" he said, annoyed at the tattered man. The shame he felt at his actions made him yell at his only friend.

"Well, goodness knows I don't want to bother anybody," the other said. There was a little sound of sadness in his voice. "Goodness knows, I've got enough of my own to worry about."

Henry, who had been thinking to himself and glancing at the tattered man with hatred, spoke in a hard voice.

"Good-bye," he said.

The tattered man looked at him in amazement.

"Why—why, partner, where are you going?" he asked unsteadily. His thoughts seemed to be swimming around in his head. "Now—now—look—here, you. Now—I won't have this—this won't do. Where—where are you going?"

Henry pointed.

"Over there," he said.

"Well, now look—here—now," said the tattered man, rambling. His head was hanging forward and he slurred his words. "This thing won't do, now. I know you. You want to go walking away with a bad wound. It's not right. You should let me take care of you. It's not right for you to go—walking off—with a bad wound—it's not—not right—it's not."

Henry climbed a fence and started running away. He could hear the tattered man calling after him, but he kept going. Once he had gotten some distance away, he turned and saw the tattered man wandering around in the field.

Henry wished he had been hurt in the battle. The simple question the tattered man had asked him was like an injury. He knew he wouldn't be able to hide his secret. Everybody would know that he had run from the fight. He couldn't even protect himself from simple questions.

CHAPTER 13

A Second Chance to Join the War

⌒

All of a sudden Henry became aware that the roar of the battle was growing louder. Great brown clouds floated past him, and the noise was getting closer. As he reached the top of a hill, he saw that the road was now crowded with wagons, teams, and men. Fear was moving everyone along.

Henry felt comforted by this sight. They were all fleeing. Perhaps, then, he wasn't so bad after all. He sat by the road and watched everyone pass. They ran like young, uncomfortable animals, and he found some pleasure in watching this wild march.

Soon a group of infantry soldiers appeared in the road. They came on swiftly and moved around everything that was in the way. These soldiers were going forward into the heart of the battle. They were ready to face the eager rush of the enemy. Their faces were serious, and Henry could tell that they felt important.

As Henry looked at them, the weight of his sadness returned to him. He felt as if he was watching a line of soldiers who had been specially chosen to be heroes. He could never be like them. He could have cried right then.

Henry wished he could be a hero, and for a moment he was about to get up and join them on their way to the fight. Then the difficulties of his situation began to drag at him and he hesitated.

He had no rifle, but there were a lot of those around. He could always pick one up. Also, he thought, it would be hard to find his own troop again. But then again, he could fight with any troop. He started forward slowly, struggling with his doubts.

Eventually Henry's objections beat out his courage. In the end, he wasn't very upset about his decision. As he thought about it, he decided that the problems were pretty big. And now, on top of everything else, new problems began to bother him.

He had a horrible thirst. His face was so dry that he thought the skin would crack. Each bone in his body had an ache in it, and his feet were sore. His stomach hurt from hunger, and he was having trouble seeing clearly. Henry realized he would never become a hero. He groaned from sadness and went wandering away.

He stayed close to the battle. He had a great desire to see the fighting and get news. He wanted to know who was winning.

It occurred to Henry that if his army lost, it might mean good things for him. Many brave men, he thought, would have to run if the army was beaten by the enemy. He would just look like another one of those men. No one would know that he had run earlier.

If they lost, it would be a kind of proof that he had done the right thing by running. It would show that he had been able to see what would happen, as if he could see the future. That kind of proof was very important to Henry. He couldn't accept the idea that he had done something shameful.

But if his army was to win, Henry would be in trouble. He knew it was awful to think these things, and he called himself a villain just for thinking about them.

Then another thought came to him. True, a defeat of his army was a way for him to escape from what he had done, but he decided that it was useless to think of such a possibility. He knew his army could never be beaten.

Henry tried to think of a good story to tell the men in his troop. He thought up many ideas, but threw each one away as too weak and unbelievable.

He imagined the whole troop making fun of him for running from the fight.

"Where's Henry Fleming?" they would ask. "He ran, didn't he? Oh, my!"

Henry imagined that he would see people staring at him with hatred wherever he went in camp. Everyone would laugh meanly at him and he would become a joke.

CHAPTER 14

A War Wound

The soldiers who had pushed their way along the road were barely out of sight when Henry saw many more men coming out of the woods and down through the fields. He knew at once that they were running for their lives. They charged past him like terrified buffaloes. Behind them smoke curled and clouded above the treetops and the cannons boomed.

Henry was stricken with terror. He stared at the sight in front of him in amazement. The fight was lost. Soon he was in the middle of the running men. He tried to ask questions of the ones closest to him, but they didn't seem to hear him. Men were running in every direction. Finally Henry grabbed one man by the arm and they swung around face to face.

"Why—why—" stammered Henry.

"Let go of me! Let go of me!" the man screamed. He was panting and he tugged frantically. "Let go!"

"Why—why—" Henry stuttered.

"Well, fine then!" the man yelled. He hit Henry in the head and ran away.

Henry fell down and found that it was hard to get back up. When he finally did, he felt very weak. There was a loud noise in his head. At last he managed to move over to the grass. He could feel a wound on the top of his head.

Henry saw that some of the soldiers and officers were trying to group themselves back into ranks. The blue haze of evening was on the field. The forest was covered with long purple shadows, and there was one cloud in the sky. Henry left the scene behind him. As he did, he heard the guns suddenly begin to roar again.

CHAPTER 15

A Helpful Stranger

Henry hurried on in the dusk. After a while, his wound stopped hurting. He thought of home as he walked, and he was eventually overcome with weariness. His head hung forward and his shoulders hunched as if he was carrying a heavy bundle. His feet scraped along the ground.

At last he heard a cheery voice near his shoulder. "You seem to be in a pretty bad way, huh?"

Henry did not look up, but he managed to say, "Uh."

The owner of the cheery voice took him firmly by the arm.

"Well," he said with a laugh, "I'm going your way. The whole gang is going your way, and I guess I can give you a lift."

As they went along, the man asked Henry what he had seen and told him what he had learned of Henry's troop.

"They're way over there in the center of the fight," the man said. "I guess just about everybody has had his share of fighting today. I almost gave up a few times. There was shooting and yelling everywhere. It was dark and I couldn't tell where I was or even what side I was on. How did you find your way over here, anyway? Your troop is pretty far from here. Well, I guess I can find them."

In the search that followed, the man with the cheery voice seemed to have some kind of magic skill. He was able to find his way easily through the maze of the tangled forest. Whenever they came across other people, the man was as smart as a detective and as brave as a hero. Problems fell away before him and became things that could help them on their way. Henry stood by while his companion found the way back for both of them.

The forest seemed to be filled with men running around in circles, lost. But the cheery man led Henry through everything until, at last, he started to chuckle with joy and satisfaction.

"Ah, there you are. See that fire?" the man asked.

Henry nodded. He felt stupid.

"Well, there's your troop," the man said. "And now, good-bye, old boy. Good luck to you."

A warm and strong hand held Henry's soft fingers for a minute, and then he heard a cheerful whistling as the man walked away. The man had been kind to him, and as he watched him walk away, Henry suddenly realized that he had never even seen the man's face.

CHAPTER 16

Return to Camp

Henry went slowly toward the fire, thinking fearfully of the welcome his friends would give him. He was sure they would make fun of him. He thought about going off into the darkness to hide, but he was too tired and sore.

He could see men sleeping on the ground near the fire. Suddenly a tall, dark figure approached him with a rifle.

"Halt! Halt!" the figure commanded.

Henry was confused for a moment, and then he thought he recognized the voice.

"Why, hello," he said. "Wilson, is—is that you?"

The rifle lowered and Wilson slowly came forward and looked into Henry's face.

"That you, Henry?" Wilson asked. "Well, old boy, I'm glad to see you. I gave you up for sure."

Henry could barely stand, and he tried to tell his story quickly.

"Yes, yes, I've had an awful time," he said. "I've been all over. I was separated from the troop, and then I got shot right here in the head—it grazed me. I've never seen such fighting. It was awful. I don't know how I got separated from the troop."

"What, shot?" Wilson stepped forward quickly. "Why didn't you say so right away? Poor old boy."

Then a corporal approached out of the darkness.

"Henry, you're here?" the corporal said. "Why, I thought you were gone four hours ago.

My goodness, they keep turning up every few minutes. We thought we had lost forty-two men, but they keep coming back. We'll have the whole company back by morning, at this rate. Where were you?"

"I got separated——" Henry started to say.

Then Wilson interrupted, "Yes, and he's been shot in the head. We have to look after him right away."

Wilson and the corporal took Henry to a blanket near the fire. The other soldiers began to help when they saw him, too. The corporal wrapped the wound on Henry's head.

As he rested, Henry looked at the other soldiers around the fire. Some were sleeping while still holding their guns and swords. All were covered with mud and dirt, and their clothes were torn. Everyone looked dead tired.

Henry sat in a sad little heap until Wilson came back swinging two canteens.

"Well, now, Henry old boy," he said. "We'll have you fixed up in a minute."

He fussed around the fire and stirred the sticks. Then he made Henry drink from the canteen that contained cold coffee. Henry drank long, and it soothed his throat. Having finished, he sighed with comfortable delight. Then Wilson wrapped Henry's head in a large handkerchief.

There," he said, looking at his work. "You look like the devil, but I bet you feel better. You're strong, Henry. You didn't yell or anything while we cleaned you up, and a shot in the head is serious. Now you lay down and get some rest."

Henry got down carefully, stretching out with a murmur of relief and comfort. The ground felt like a soft couch.

But suddenly he sat up and said, "Hold on a minute. Where are you going to sleep?"

His friend waved away his question.

"Right down there by you," he said.

"What are you going to sleep in? I've got your blanket."

"Be quiet and go on to sleep," Wilson snarled. "Don't make a fool of yourself."

At that, Henry was silent. A sense of sleepiness had spread through his whole body. Under the warm comfort of the blanket, his head fell forward onto his arm and his eyelids quickly closed. Hearing some gunfire in the distance, Henry wondered if those men ever slept. He gave a long sigh, snuggled down into his blanket, and in a moment was just like his friends.

CHAPTER 17

A Fight at Camp

ᐁ

Whe Henry woke up it seemed to him that
he had been asleep for a thousand years. An icy
dew had chilled his face, and he stared for a while
at the leaves that blew around overhead. In the
distance he could hear the sound of fighting.

Around him were groups of sleeping men,
motionless, pale, and in strange positions. For a
brief moment he thought that they were all
dead. Then he saw Wilson warming up by a small
fire. A few other figures moved in the fog, and he
heard someone chopping wood.

Suddenly there was the rumble of drums, and a distant bugle sounded faintly. The men around him began to get up. Wilson saw that Henry was awake and asked, "Well, Henry, old man, how do you feel this morning?"

Henry yawned. His head felt like a melon, and his stomach hurt.

"Oh, I feel pretty bad," he said.

Wilson fixed the bandage on Henry's head, and then prepared some food for both of them. Henry remembered how differently his friend had behaved before their big battle. He was not a loud young soldier anymore. He was quiet and sure of himself, and he didn't get upset at the little things other men said to him. Henry wondered when this change had come over his friend.

Wilson balanced his coffee cup on his knee and said, "Well, Henry, what do you think our chances are? Do you think we'll beat them?"

Henry thought for a while and then said, "The day before yesterday, you would have said you could beat them all by yourself."

Wilson looked amazed.

"Would I have said that?" he asked. "Well, maybe I would. I believe I was a pretty big fool before all this."

Henry tried to apologize for embarrassing his friend, but Wilson waved it away. After a while, Wilson said that they had the enemy right where they wanted them.

"I don't know about that," Henry said. "From where I was yesterday, it looked like we were getting hit pretty hard."

"Do you think so?" Wilson asked. "I thought we handled them pretty rough yesterday."

"Not a bit," said Henry. "Why, you didn't see anything of the fight."

All around them were other small fires surrounded by men. From one of these suddenly came sharp voices. Two soldiers had been teasing a huge, bearded man, who had become upset. It looked now as if there would be a fight.

Wilson stood up and broke the men apart.

"Here now, boys," he said. "What's the use of this? We'll be fighting the enemy in less than an hour. Why fight among ourselves?"

One of the other soldiers reminded Wilson that he had been in a fistfight a few days ago and had lost.

"You just don't like fighting since you lost that one," the soldier said. "Besides, this is none of your business."

Eventually the men's argument quieted down and Wilson returned to his seat. Soon, all the men were joking with each other like old friends.

"I hate to see the boys fighting among themselves," Wilson said.

Henry laughed and said, "You've changed a

lot. I remember when you would have fought anyone without even thinking about it."

"I guess I used to be that way," Wilson said.

"I'm sorry if I'm embarrassing you," Henry said, after a moment.

"Oh, don't worry about it, Henry," Wilson said. He thought for a while, and then said, "We thought the troop lost over half the men yesterday. I thought they were all gone, but they kept coming back last night until it looked like we only lost a few. They had been scattered all over the place, fighting with other troops, just like you did."

"Is that so?" Henry asked.

CHAPTER 18

The Letter

∽

The troop was standing at attention at the side of a road, waiting for the command to march. Suddenly Henry remembered the little packet wrapped in a faded yellow envelope that Wilson had given him the other day.

"Wilson," Henry called to his friend.

"What?"

Wilson was staring down the road. For some strange reason, the look on his face at that moment made him appear very frightened. Henry felt that he should change the subject.

"Oh, nothing," Henry said.

He decided not to remind him of the other day, when Wilson had felt so scared and certain that he was going to die that he gave Henry the envelope. To remind him of that moment of fear would just be mean.

Henry used to be afraid of Wilson, for it used to be so easy to upset him. But now, Henry had a new plan. If Wilson asked him about what had really happened the previous day—if he discovered that Henry had actually run from battle— then Henry would bring out the little envelope and remind him of how scared he had been. It was like a weapon he could use to protect himself from being laughed at.

In a rare weak moment, Wilson had spoken with sobs of his own death. He had given Henry the envelope, which probably held keepsakes for his relatives. Now Henry felt that he was better than his friend. He even felt sorry for Wilson.

Henry now had his pride back. Yes, he had made mistakes, but no one would ever know about them. He was still a man. He did not think about the battles that were coming soon. He would not have to plan how he would deal with them. He had learned yesterday that he would not be punished for avoiding his duties.

Besides, he was now feeling confident. He had more faith in himself. He was now a man of experience. He had been in danger, had seen the worst that could happen, and now believed that it was not that bad.

Anyway, Henry thought, how could they kill him when it was obvious that he had been chosen for greatness? How else could he have survived everything that had happened already?

He remembered how some of the other men had run from the battle. As he thought about their terror-filled faces, he felt that he didn't like them. They had been weak and had run too quickly, when everyone could see them. He had run secretly and with pride.

Wilson coughed loudly and brought him back from his daydreaming.

"Henry," he said.

"What?" asked Henry.

Wilson coughed again. He moved around as if he was uncomfortable.

"Well," he said at last. His face was red. "I guess you can give me back that letter."

"All right, Wilson," Henry said after a few moments.

He opened his jacket and removed the letter from his inside pocket. He gave it to Wilson, who was so embarrassed that he couldn't even look at Henry.

Henry had done this slowly because he was thinking of something to say about the letter. But he couldn't think of anything to say, so instead he decided he would be nice and not tease his friend.

After this, Henry thought again about the battles he had seen so far. He was sure that he could now return home and make people's hearts glow with stories of war. He could see himself in a room telling tales to listeners. He saw his audience imagining him as the hero in all kinds of blazing scenes.

CHAPTER 19

On the Move

⎯⎯⎯⎯

This part of the world led a strange, battle-filled existence. The roar of gunfire could always be heard, and the cannons made a thudding sound in the fog.

Henry's troop was ordered to take over for a troop that had been lying in some damp trenches for a long time. All around them were the sounds of fighting. The noise came from the woods ahead of them and to their left. The sounds to their right grew worse with each passing minute. It soon became impossible to hear anyone speak.

Henry wanted to make a joke, but no one would have heard him. At last, the guns stopped and the rumors began to fly among the men again. The men talked about other battles, disasters that had been lost.

When the guns started up again, the men were unhappy and began to mutter. They made gestures that said "Ah, what more can we do?" They had heard stories that their army was losing the war.

Before the fog cleared, the troop was marching carefully through the woods. Enemy men could sometimes be seen hurrying through the trees and little fields. They were yelling—excited and happy.

At this sight, Henry became angry and yelled, "We're being controlled by a lot of lunkheads!"

"More than one man has said that today," said one of his friends.

Henry started to complain loudly about

the commander of their army, but Wilson stopped him.

"Maybe it wasn't all his fault," said Wilson in a tired voice. "He did the best he could. It's our bad luck to get beaten by them."

"Well, don't we fight like the devil?" Henry said loudly. "Don't we do all that men can?"

He was secretly amazed that he had said this. For a moment he felt guilty, but no one questioned his right to speak this way and his courage returned soon enough.

"Nobody would ever say we don't fight hard," said Wilson. "But still, we haven't had any luck."

"Well, then, if we fight so well, it must be the general's fault," said Henry. "I don't see any sense in fighting all the time and always losing because of some lunkhead of a general."

A man who was walking beside him said, "Maybe you think you fought the whole army yesterday, Henry."

At that, Henry was quiet. He was afraid that the others would ask him for more details of what had happened to him the previous day. He didn't want to draw any more attention to himself.

The troops at last halted in a clear space. There were battle noises all around them.

"We're always being chased around like rats," Henry grumbled. "Nobody knows where we go or why we go. We just get moved around. Now the enemy has had all the time to get ready for us, and we just arrived. Don't tell me, it's bad luck. I know better. It's this darn old—"

Wilson interrupted him in a calm, confident voice. "It'll turn out all right in the end."

The day had become brighter, and the sun shone its full brightness upon the forest. A single rifle flashed in the woods in front of the troop. In less than a minute it was joined by many others. A mighty roar of clashes and crashes went sweeping through the woods. The battle noise became a rolling thunder filled with long explosions.

The men in the troop waited. They were worn out. They had not slept much, and they had worked a lot. They looked at the approaching battle and waited for the shock. Some moved back a little, flinching at the sounds. The rest stood like men tied to posts.

CHAPTER 20

A Real Hero

⌒

Seeing the enemy come at them, Henry felt a sudden sense of rage. He stamped his feet and glared with hatred at the swirling smoke that was approaching. It made him mad that the enemy wouldn't let him rest, wouldn't give him any time to sit down and think. Yesterday he had fought and fled quickly. There had been many adventures. He felt that he had earned the right to have a rest. He was exhausted.

But those other men seemed never to get tired, and he had a wild hatred for them. Henry

didn't want to be chased anymore. He bent down behind a little tree and clenched his teeth. The bandage was still wrapped around his head. Over his wound there was a small spot of blood. His hair was messed and hung over the cloth bandage, covering his forehead. His jacket and shirt were open at the throat. His fingers were wrapped nervously around his rifle. He felt that the enemy was insulting him and his friends. They were being treated as if they were poor and puny, and he wanted revenge. He wanted to beat them.

One rifle flashed in front of them, followed instantly by others. A moment later his troop started firing back. A thick wall of smoke settled over everything. Henry was fighting hard. He didn't even know if he was standing. When he lost his balance and fell, he jumped back up right away. His rifle barrel became so hot that he wouldn't have been able to hold it on any other day. But today he kept shooting.

He fought and fought. He kept firing his gun even when everyone around him had stopped. He was so focused on fighting that he didn't notice how quiet it had become. Finally he heard a loud laugh and a voice that sounded amazed.

"You fool!" someone yelled. "Don't you know enough to stop when there's nothing left to shoot at?"

Henry turned and looked at his friends. They were all staring at him in surprise. When he looked to the front again, he saw a deserted field under the smoke. He looked confused for a moment, then realized what he was seeing.

"Oh," he said.

Henry returned to his friends and lay heavily on the ground. The lieutenant was yelling excitedly, and called out to him, "If I had ten thousand wildcats like you I could win this war in a week!"

Some of the men muttered and looked at Henry in amazement. Wilson came walking over to him and asked, "Are you all right, Fleming? Do you feel all right? There's nothing wrong with you, Henry, is there?"

"No," Henry said with some difficulty.

He realized he had fought like an animal, and that it hadn't been hard. He had struggled to overcome his fear, and now he was what he would call a hero. He hadn't even noticed it happening.

He lay on the ground and enjoyed the other men staring at him from time to time. Their faces were dirty with gunpowder. They were all sweating and breathing hard.

"Hot work!" the lieutenant said loudly. He was very happy with the troop's performance, and walked up and down among the men. He was restless and eager. Sometimes he would even laugh.

"By thunder," one of the men said. "I bet this army will never see another troop like us!"

"You bet!" said another.

"The more you press us, the tougher we get," said someone.

"They lost a pile of men," said a soldier.

"Yes, and if they come back they'll lose a lot more," said someone else.

There was still noise in the forest. From far off in the trees came the rolling clatter of gunfire. A dark cloud of smoke went up toward the sun, now bright in the blue sky.

CHAPTER 21

The Conversation

The ragged line of soldiers had a few minutes' rest, but the sounds of fighting in the forest kept becoming louder and louder. The trees seemed to quiver and the ground to shake from the rushing of the men. Henry's troop listened quietly to the noise.

Everyone was thirsty. Wilson said that he had heard of a stream nearby, so he volunteered to go for some water. Henry offered to help. Immediately canteens were showered on them.

"Fill mine, will you?" said one man.

"Bring me some, too," said another.

"Me, too," said others.

Henry and Wilson left, weighed down with several canteens. They searched for a while, but when they couldn't find the stream they decided to head back.

From their position, they could see more of the battle than when they were with their troop. They could see many dark clouds of smoke, where other troops were fighting. Over some trees, they saw part of a house that was burning and sending smoke far into the sky. They saw their own troops, too. Behind them the hill was crowded with troops who were pulling back.

Looking into the forest nearby, Henry and Wilson saw a general and his staff riding on horses. They passed a wounded soldier without stopping. A moment later, another officer rode his horse right up to the general. No one seemed to notice Henry and his friend, so they stayed nearby and tried to overhear what the general was saying.

"The enemy's forming over there for another charge," the general said. He spoke calmly, as if he was talking about the officer's clothes. "I fear they'll break through unless we work like thunder to stop them."

"It'll be hard to stop them," the officer said, angrily.

"I expect so," the general said. Then he began to talk quickly and quietly among his staff. Henry and Wilson could hear nothing until the general finally asked the officer, "What troops can you spare?"

"Well," the officer said, thinking. "There's the 304th. They're useless. Fight like a lot of mule drivers. I can spare them easily enough."

Henry and Wilson looked at each other in amazement. The 304th was their troop. The general spoke sharply. "Get them ready then. I'll watch

the battle from here and send word of when to start them. It'll be over in five minutes. I don't believe many of your mule drivers will survive this."

The officer and the general smiled as they parted. With scared faces, Henry and Wilson hurried back to their troop. Even though this happened in just a few minutes, Henry felt as if he had aged many years.

He learned that he did not mean anything to the army. The officer had spoken about their troop as if he had been talking about a broom. When they got back, they told everyone that they were going to charge at the enemy in minutes.

"Charge?" said their lieutenant, with a smile. "Well, then, now we're fighting!"

The men saw two figures on horseback a short distance from them. One was the colonel of the troop. The other was the officer who had received his orders from the general. They were talking and pointing at the troop.

The officers began to move the men into smaller groups. Soon, everyone in the troop seemed to stand up straight and take a deep breath. They were watching the forest. All around them were the noises of a great battle between the two armies. The rest of the world seemed to be interested in other things. The troop had this little fight all to itself.

Henry and Wilson looked at each other. They hadn't told anyone how the officer and general had spoken about the troop, about how they were all men whose lives didn't matter very much. They had been called mule drivers, Henry thought. They weren't expected to survive this fight. But that was a secret between Henry and Wilson. Still, they could see the fear in each other's faces. They looked at each other and nodded in agreement when a man near them said in a frightened voice, "We'll get swallowed."

CHAPTER 22

Across the Field

Henry stared at the land in front of him. The trees seemed to hide all kinds of horrors. He didn't know when the troop started to charge, but from the corner of his eye he saw an officer on horseback riding forward. Suddenly Henry felt the men stir, and the troop moved slowly forward like a wall falling over. Henry was pushed for a moment before he understood what was happening. He jumped and started to run desperately. He looked like an insane soldier.

From the line of trees came the yells of the

enemy and little flames of gunfire. Men were falling all around Henry. Soon the troop had run into a clearing. Henry could see everything more clearly: every blade of grass, every brown tree trunk, and the faces of the soldiers, their staring eyes and sweating faces.

After running for what seemed like miles, the troop slowed and finally stopped. Almost at once, the distant sound of gunfire became a roar. Long fingers of smoke spread out around them.

Having stopped, the men could now see the ones who had fallen, or were injured and yelling. For an instant, the men appeared dazed and unable to move. It was a strange pause and a strange silence. Then, above all other sounds came the roar of the lieutenant. "Come on, you fools!" he screamed. "Come on! You can't stay here. You must keep moving!" He said more, but most of it could not be understood.

The men just stared at him while he continued

to yell. Finally, Wilson jumped forward and dropped to his knees. He fired his gun into the woods. This seemed to wake the other men and they stopped huddling together like sheep. They seemed to remember their weapons and started firing all at once. Cheered on by their officers, the men began to move forward slowly, stopping every few paces to fire and reload.

The enemy was fighting hard to keep the troop from advancing, and it felt as if they couldn't move anymore. The men bent down behind some trees and held on as if threatened by a wave. They looked wild-eyed at each other, as if amazed at what they had caused. The whole situation was very confusing to many of them.

As soon as they stopped, the lieutenant started yelling at them again. He grabbed Henry by the arm and cried, "Come on, you lunkhead! We'll all get shot if we stay here. We've only got to cross that field there."

"Cross there?" Henry said, pointing.

"Yes, just cross that field! We can't stay here," screamed the lieutenant. "Come on!"

They ran together, with Wilson running after them. All three men yelled at their troop. "Come on! Come on!"

The troop hesitated for a moment. Then, with a long cry, they ran forward and began their new journey. Over the field, the handful of men left in the troop moved closer to the enemy. The gunfire came even faster, and a huge cloud of blue smoke hung over them.

Henry ran to reach the woods before a bullet could find him. He ducked his head low. His eyes were almost closed. The scene around him was a wild blur.

As he pushed himself forward, he found that he felt love and a sad fondness for the flag that was near him. He believed now that it was beautiful and powerful. Surely no harm could ever come to it. He kept close to it, as if it could protect him.

In the mad scramble, he saw the soldier carrying the flag flinch suddenly and fall.

Henry jumped and clutched at the flag pole. At the same instant, Wilson grabbed it from the other side.

CHAPTER 23

The Flag

ৎ৵

When the two youths turned with the flag, they saw that much of the troop was gone. Not only that, but the survivors were starting to pull back. Several officers were giving orders, screaming over the noise of the battle.

"Where are you going?" the lieutenant cried.

Henry and Wilson had a small fight over the flag. Each of them wanted to carry it. Finally, Henry pushed Wilson away.

The troop moved back into the trees. By the time they had returned to the open space where they had started, there seemed to be mobs of enemy soldiers all around them. Most of the men in the troop were surprised and discouraged.

Henry kept moving, a look of rage on his face. He was angry that they had been called mule drivers, and even angrier that they were now forced to pull back. He hated that officer who didn't even know him, but had called him a mule driver. Henry had wanted his troop to win this battle. He wanted to return to that officer and say, "So, we're mule drivers, are we?" But now Henry knew they were not going to win, and he had to let go of his dreams for revenge.

Henry wrapped himself in his pride and kept the flag high. He and the lieutenant yelled at the troop to keep fighting, but the men were like a worn down machine. Many of the soldiers could not continue when they saw others falling and wounded.

There was smoke everywhere. Through a

sudden break in a cloud, Henry saw a group of enemy troops. They yelled and began firing as Henry's troop pulled back.

The battle seemed to take forever. In the haze, some soldiers panicked and got lost. Many of them headed in the wrong direction. Soldiers became confused about where the enemy was and where gunfire was coming from. Men ran in every direction, looking for ways to escape. All the while, with almost regular timing, men continued to fall.

Very sure of himself, Henry walked into the middle of the mob and took a stand with the flag. It was as if he expected someone to push him to the ground, and he was using the flag to hold himself up. Without knowing it, he was posed like the heroes he had seen and imagined.

Wilson came up to him and said, "Well, Henry, I guess this is good-bye."

"Oh shut up, you darned fool!" Henry replied. He would not look at his friend.

The officers worked to get the troop into a circle. They wanted the men to face the approaching enemy. The ground was uneven and torn. The men crawled into ditches and tried to hide behind anything that might stop a bullet.

Henry saw that the lieutenant was standing quietly now. He was using his sword like a cane to hold himself up. There was something strange in this little pause. The lieutenant looked like a child who had cried all he could and now didn't know what to do. He was thinking and mumbling to himself.

Some lazy smoke curled slowly around the troop. The men hiding from the bullets waited for it to lift so they could see once and for all what would happen to them.

CHAPTER 24

A Brief Victory

ᨕ

Suddenly, the men's silence was broken by the eager voice of the lieutenant, who yelled, "Here they come!" The rest of his words were lost in the roar of thunder from the men's rifles.

Henry looked to where the lieutenant had pointed and saw the enemy soldiers closing in. They were so near that he could see their faces. Their gray uniforms seemed new.

These troops had been advancing with caution, their rifles ready to shoot. When the lieutenant yelled and Henry's troop started shooting,

the enemy soldiers seemed surprised and were caught unaware.

The two troops traded blows like boxers. The fast, angry gunfire went back and forth. Henry's troop, in blue uniforms, were desperate for revenge. Henry ducked and dodged for a time. He had a few poor views of the enemy soldiers. There appeared to be many of them, and they seemed to be moving forward, step by step. Henry sat gloomily on the ground with the flag between his knees.

As he noticed the wolflike anger of his friends, he thought that if the enemy soldiers were indeed going to win, it would be a painful victory.

But the blows of the enemy began to grow weak. Fewer bullets ripped the air. Finally, when the men slowed a bit to take a look around, they could see only the dark, floating smoke. The troop lay still and stared at the space around them. Except for the fallen bodies, the ground was empty of enemy soldiers.

At the sight of this, many of the men in blue jumped up from beneath their covers and made a strange dance of joy. Their eyes burned and a hoarse cheer broke from their dry lips.

They had almost believed that they were useless and that they could not fight well. On the edge of losing this small battle, they learned that the size of the army was not important. They had gotten revenge on the enemy and won.

They looked around with pride and felt trust in the grim weapons they held. And they were men.

CHAPTER 25

The General's Opinion

⌒

There was open space around them. In the distance there were many loud noises, but in this part of the field there was sudden stillness. They thought they were free. The small band of soldiers drew a long breath of relief and gathered together to return to their lines, where the rest of their army camped.

In this last part of their journey, the men began to show strange emotions. They hurried on, very anxious. Some of the men who had not shown any emotion in the middle of the fight now could not hide their nervousness. Perhaps they were worried about being shot now, after the main battle was over and when they were so close to safety.

As they approached their lines, soldiers in a troop that they passed made fun of Henry and his friends.

"Where have you been?" one soldier yelled at them.

"Why didn't you stay out there?" called another.

"Going home now, boys?" yelled a third.

There was no reply from the bruised troop, except for one man who challenged the others to fistfights. But the lieutenant prevented that from happening. Henry was angry over those remarks. He saw that many in his troop walked as if they felt guilty, moving along with sudden heaviness.

They turned around when they arrived at

their old position and looked at the ground where they had charged. Henry was astonished. The distances were tiny. It amazed him that so much had happened in such a small space, and he began to feel proud of his actions during the recent battle.

As the troop lay resting, the officer who had called them mule drivers came riding along the line. He had lost his cap, and his hair flew wildly. His face was dark with anger. He immediately began yelling at the troop.

"Oh, thunder," he screamed. "What an awful mess you made of this thing! You stopped about a hundred feet away from a great success. If you men had gone a hundred feet farther, you would have made a great charge."

The men now turned to look at their colonel. He was about to speak. He looked as if he had been insulted. Then his manner changed suddenly, and he shrugged his shoulders.

"Oh, well, general, we went as far as we could," he said calmly.

"As far as you could?" yelled the officer. "Well, that wasn't very far, was it? You were supposed to draw away the enemy's attention and you failed completely."

Then he turned his horse and rode away. The colonel muttered angry words to himself. The lieutenant, who had listened with quiet rage to the general, now spoke loudly. "I don't care what a man is—whether he's a general or any other rank. If he says the boys didn't put up a good fight, he's a fool."

CHAPTER 26

Major Generals

୧ଠ

T he news that the troop had been called a failure went along the line. The other troops all said the general had made a huge mistake. Henry saw that his friends looked like beaten animals. Wilson looked at him and said, "I wonder what he wants from us. He must think we went out there and played marbles!"

Although he was angry, Henry decided to stay calm.

"Oh, well," he said. "The general probably didn't see any of it. He probably got mad and decided that we were a lot of sheep, just because we didn't do exactly what he wanted done. It's just our awful luck, that's all."

"I should say so," replied his friend. He seemed deeply insulted. "There's no fun in fighting for people when everything you do—no matter what—isn't done right. I almost want to stay behind next time. Let them take their charge and go to the devil with it."

Just then several men came hurrying up.

"Oh, Fleming, you have to hear this!" cried one of them.

"Hear what?" asked Henry.

"Well, the colonel met with your lieutenant right near us, and he said, 'Who was that lad who carried the flag?' Then the lieutenant says, 'That's Henry Fleming. He's a tough kid.' Those were his exact words. And the colonel says, 'He is, indeed. He is a very good man to have. He kept the flag right up at the front. I saw him. He's a good one all right.' Then the lieutenant said, 'You bet. He and a fellow named Wilson were at the head of the charge the whole time.' Then the colonel said, 'Well, well, they deserve to be major generals.'"

Henry and Wilson were blushing from the thrill of hearing this news. They shared a secret glance of joy and congratulation. Soon they forgot many things. The past held no disappointments. They were very happy. Their hearts swelled with grateful affection for the colonel and their lieutenant.

CHAPTER 27

The Second Attack

⌒

When the enemy again began to charge from the woods, Henry felt completely sure of himself. While others ducked and dodged, he stood tall and calm. He watched as the attack began against a part of his army that was on the side of a nearby hill. In another part of the field, two other troops were fighting hard and fast. They seemed to be ignoring the other battles going on around them.

In another direction, he saw a wonderful group on horseback going into the woods. They passed out of sight and soon there was a loud and shocking noise. Henry watched the small battles, which went on for some time. The troops struck fiercely and powerfully at each other. He could see the flags shaking in the smoke.

Soon everything became still again. The hush was serious and churchlike. Suddenly the guns on a nearby slope roared out. The sound of gunfire had begun in the woods. It grew with amazing speed until it was unbelievably loud. Henry could hear nothing else.

Men were rushing back and forth everywhere he looked. Sometimes the men from one army would yell and cheer, but a moment later the other side would cheer just as much. Everywhere, the men screamed and yelled.

Henry's small troop charged forward just as fiercely as ever when their time came. The men burst out in a cry of rage and pain when the enemy shot at them. The front of Henry's troop was a wall of smoke. They could see only the flashing points of yellow and red gunfire. The men quickly became covered in dirt and grime.

The lieutenant continued to yell and scream at his men to keep them fighting. Henry still carried the flag. He tried to see all he could. Sometimes he flinched or talked to himself. Sometimes he did not even know if he was breathing. He was so busy watching the battles.

A big line of enemy soldiers came within dangerous range. They could be seen easily. They were tall, skinny men with excited faces, and they ran with long strides. At this sight, Henry's troop fell silent for a moment before they began shooting. They hadn't even been ordered to start firing. They just started as soon as they realized the danger they were in.

But the enemy was quick to take cover behind a fence. Once there, they began firing back at Henry's troop, which prepared itself for a great struggle. White clenched teeth shone from the dirty faces. The enemy often shouted and tried to insult them, but Henry's troop remained silent. Perhaps they were remembering the general's insult, which made them fight even harder.

Henry had decided not to move, whatever should happen. He wanted revenge on the officer who had called them mule drivers and fail-

ures. The best revenge he could think of was to stay there until the enemy was beaten. He would show everyone how brave he was.

The troop was hurt badly, and many men fell. Some of the wounded crawled away from the battle, but many lay still.

Henry looked for and found Wilson, who was still fighting. The lieutenant was also unhurt. He had continued to yell at the men, but it was different now. They were firing less and less, and the lieutenant's voice was quickly growing weak.

CHAPTER 28

The Other Side of the Fence

༄

The colonel came running along the back of the line, with other officers following him.

"We must charge them!" they shouted. "We must charge them!"

When he heard this, Henry began to study the distance between him and the enemy. He knew that his troop would have to go forward if they were going to be good soldiers. It would be death to stay where they were. Their only hope was to push the enemy away from the fence where they were hiding.

He thought his companions would be too tired to charge, and they would have to be encouraged. But when he turned to look at them, he saw with surprise that they were giving quick and sure expressions of agreement. When the command came, the soldiers sprang forward in eager leaps. There was a new and unexpected force in their movements. They knew they were tired, and the energy of this charge was like the strength that comes just before the end. The men ran in an insane fever. It was a blind rush over a green field and under and blue sky toward a fence dimly outlined in smoke. Behind the fence, the enemy was shooting right at them.

Henry kept the flag at the front. He was waving his free arm in great circles and yelling. He tried to urge on his friends, but they didn't seem to need it. The men had grown wild with enthusiasm.

Henry also felt a daring spirit, and was ready to make huge sacrifices. He had no time to think, but he knew that the enemy bullets were the only things that might keep him from reaching his goal.

CHAPTER 29

Capturing the Flag

❦

Henry pushed forward with all his strength. He couldn't see anything except the smoke, but he knew that the old fence was there. It must have belonged to a farmer once, but now it belonged to the enemy soldiers.

As he ran, the thought of the final contact between his troop and the enemy sparkled in his mind. He expected an explosion when the two bodies of troops crashed together. It made him run faster than his friends, who were giving hoarse and frantic cheers.

But soon he could see that many of the enemy soldiers were not going to stay for the fight. As the smoke moved, Henry saw enemy men running away. Some of them turned back often to fire at Henry's troop before continuing to flee.

But at one part of the enemy line, there was a grim and determined group who did not move. They were settled firmly down behind the fence. A flag, ruffled and fierce, waved over them.

Henry's troop got closer and closer, until the two groups of soldiers could yell to each other. The cries of the two parties were now an exchange of insults. The space between them decreased almost to nothing.

Henry focused his gaze on the enemy flag. He wanted it more than anything else. He charged like a mad horse at it. His own flag shook as it approached the other.

Henry's troop came to a sudden halt at close

range and fired a swift volley of bullets. The enemy split and broke up, but they still fought. Henry's troop yelled again and rushed in.

Henry saw some of the enemy men fighting to the very end. One of them carried the flag. It was a horrible battle. With a dark and grim expression, the enemy flag-bearer hugged the flag even as he stumbled and fell down. His wounds made it seem as if his steps were being held back by invisible creatures who grabbed his legs. He looked so upset as the swirling blue line leaped at the fence.

Wilson went over the fence and sprang at the flag like a panther at its prey. He pulled at it and, yanking it free, swung it up with a mad cry of excitement as the enemy flag-bearer fell to the ground.

Henry's troop began to cheer wildly.

The fight for the little hill was over! Afterward, four of the enemy soldiers were held and questioned as prisoners. One of them had an injured foot, and he yelled and cursed at the men in blue. Another was very young, and talked calmly with Henry's friends. They talked of battles and conditions. The third prisoner sat with a sad expression. He would only tell the men in blue to go to the devil. The last prisoner was always silent, and kept his face turned away from the others. He seemed to be deeply ashamed.

After the men in blue had celebrated enough, they settled down behind the fence, on the opposite side to the one where the enemy had been.

There was some long grass. Henry lay in it and rested. Wilson, joyful and full of glory, walked over to Henry with the enemy flag. They lay side by side and congratulated each other.

CHAPTER 30

A New Start

The noises around them began to grow weaker and less frequent. Henry and Wilson suddenly looked up, worried at the silence. They could see changes going on among the troops, who were marching this way and that.

Henry stood up.

"Well, what now, I wonder," he said. He seemed to be preparing for some new noise. He shaded his eyes with his dirty hand and gazed over the field.

Wilson also stood and stared.

"I bet we're going to get out of this and back over the river," he said.

They waited and watched. In a little while, the troop received orders to retrace its way. The men got up from the grass and stretched their arms over their heads. One man swore as he rubbed his eyes. They all groaned. They had as many objections to this as they would have had to a proposal for a new battle. They had been comfortable where they were.

The men marched back over the field slowly. Just a short time earlier they had run across it madly.

The troop kept walking until it joined the rest of the army. The troops reformed into columns and marched through the woods. They passed within view of a white house. In front of it were groups of their soldiers firing at a distant enemy.

At this point the troops curved away from the field and went winding off in the direction of the river. When Henry realized where they were going, he looked over his shoulder at the trampled ground and breathed deeply with satisfaction. Then he nudged Wilson and said, "Well, we're leaving the battlefield. It's all over."

Wilson gazed backward, too.

"It really is," he said, in amazement.

It took some time for Henry to adjust to this change. Slowly his brain came out of the clouds and he was able to understand where he was and what was happening. He understood that the time to fight was in the past. He had been in a land of strange battles, and had come back. He had been where there was red blood and black passion, and he had escaped. His first thoughts were to celebrate.

Later, he began to study his actions—his failures and his achievements. He felt happy and did not regret anything. Only the best of his actions had been witnessed. It was a pleasure to remember these things, and he spent a long time reliving them in his mind.

He saw that he was good. He recalled with a thrill of joy the comments of his comrades about how brave he had been.

Still, the ghost of his flight from the first battle came back to him. There were small complaints in his brain about this. He blushed for a moment, and he felt a flicker of shame.

Then the memory of the tattered soldier whom he had deserted in the field came back to him. For an instant, a chill of sweat came over him at the thought that others might know how he had behaved. He gave a cry of pain.

Wilson turned and asked, "What's the matter, Henry?"

Henry could only reply with curses muttered to himself.

As he marched, this vision of his behavior hung over him. It clung to him and darkened his good memories. Whichever way his thoughts turned, they were followed by the phantom of the tattered soldier left alone in the field. Henry looked at his friends and felt certain that they could see the guilt in his face. But they were walking away, talking about the great victory in the recent battle.

For a time, this memory of the tattered soldier took all the celebration out of Henry. He saw his mistake, and he was afraid that it would stay with him for his entire life. He didn't talk with his friends and tried not to look at any of them.

But slowly he gathered the strength to put the sin behind him. And at last, his eyes seemed to open to some new ways. He looked back at his behavior and beliefs before he had been in the battles, and he discovered that he hated the way he had been.

With this discovery came self-confidence. He felt that he had really become a strong and quiet man. He knew that he wouldn't back down from any future battles. He had been close to death and found that, after all, it was only death.

So it happened that as he trudged from the place of blood and wrath, his soul changed. He was not angry and fearful anymore.

It rained. The soldiers marched in the mud. They appeared upset and were muttering to themselves. But Henry smiled, for he saw that the world was waiting for him. He had rid himself of the sickness of battle. The nightmare was in the past. He had been an animal, blistered and sweating in the heat and pain of war. He turned now to an image of beautiful skies, fresh meadows, and cool rivers: a life of soft and unending peace.

Over the river, a golden ray of sun came through the rain clouds.

What Do *You* Think?
Questions for Discussion

⌒

Have you ever been around a toddler who keeps asking the question "Why?" Does your teacher call on you in class with questions from your homework? Do your parents ask you questions about your day at the dinner table? We are always surrounded by questions that need a specific response. But is it possible to have a question with no right answer?

The following questions are about the book

you just read. But this is not a quiz! They are designed to help you look at the people, places, and events in the story from different angles. These questions do not have specific answers. Instead, they might make you think of the story in a completely new way.

Think carefully about each question and enjoy discovering more about this classic story.

1. Henry says that he feels like the government forced him to join the army. Why do you think he feels this way? Have you ever been forced to do something you didn't want to do?

2. Did it surprise you that Henry fired the first shot of the battle? Did you expect him to fight or run before the battle started? What would you have done in his place?

3. Henry never seems to be able to make up him mind about how he feels. Have you ever known anyone like him?

4. Henry is scared that the dead man in the forest will stand up and run after him. Why do you think he is worried about this? What is the scariest thing that has ever happened to you?

5. Why do you think the tattered man's question bothers Henry so much? How would you have reacted if you were in his position?

6. Why do you suppose the soldier helps Henry find his way back to his troop? Have you ever helped a stranger? Why did you do it?

7. Henry and Wilson both find that they have been changed by their experiences in the war. Have you ever had an experience that changed you? What was it?

8. How does hearing himself called a "mule driver" affect Henry? How would you feel if you were insulted like that? Have you ever overheard something you shouldn't have?

9. Henry runs away from the second battle. Do you think he was right to do so? What would you have done in his situation?

10. By the end of the book, Henry is seen as a man of courage and honor. Do you agree with this? How would you describe Henry?

Afterword

by Arthur Pober, EdD

⤚

First impressions are important.

Whether we are meeting new people, going to new places, or picking up a book unknown to us, first impressions count for a lot. They can lead to warm, lasting memories or can make us shy away from any future encounters.

Can you recall your own first impressions and earliest memories of reading the classics?

Do you remember wading through pages and pages of text to prepare for an exam? Or were you the child who hid under the blanket to read with a flashlight, joining forces with Robin Hood to save Maid Marian? Do you remember only how long it took you to read a lengthy novel such as *Little Women*? Or did you become best friends with the March sisters?

Even for a gifted young reader, getting through long chapters with dense language can easily become overwhelming and can obscure the richness of the story and its characters. Reading an abridged, newly crafted version of a classic novel can be the gentle introduction a child needs to explore the characters and story line without the frustration of difficult vocabulary and complex themes.

Reading an abridged version of a classic novel gives the young reader a sense of independence and the satisfaction of finishing a "grown-up" book. And when a child is engaged with and inspired by a classic story, the tone is set for further exploration of the story's themes, characters, history, and details. As a child's reading skills advance, the desire to tackle the original, unabridged version of the story will naturally emerge.

If made accessible to young readers, these stories can become invaluable tools for understanding themselves in the context of their families and social environments. This is why the *Classic Starts* series includes questions that stimulate discussion regarding the impact and social relevance of the characters and stories today. These questions can foster lively conversations between children and their parents or teachers. When we look at the issues, values, and standards of past times in terms of how we live now, we can appreciate literature's classic tales in a very personal and engaging way.

Share your love of reading the classics with a young child, and introduce an imaginary world real enough to last a lifetime.

Dr. Arthur Pober, EdD

Dr. Arthur Pober has spent more than twenty years in the fields of early-childhood and gifted education. He is the former principal of one of the world's oldest laboratory schools for gifted youngsters, Hunter College Elementary School, and former Director of Magnet Schools for the Gifted and Talented for more than 25,000 youngsters in New York City.

Dr. Pober is a recognized authority in the areas of media and child protection and is currently the U.S. representative to the European Institute for the Media and European Advertising Standards Alliance.

Explore these wonderful stories in our
Classic Starts™ library.

20,000 Leagues Under the Sea

The Adventures of Huckleberry Finn

The Adventures of Robin Hood

The Adventures of Sherlock Holmes

The Adventures of Tom Sawyer

Alice in Wonderland & Through the Looking Glass

Anne of Avonlea

Anne of Green Gables

Arabian Nights

Around the World in 80 Days

Black Beauty

The Call of the Wild

Dracula

The Five Little Peppers and How They Grew

Frankenstein